My First Time

Moving Day

Kate Petty, Lisa Kopper, and Jim Pipe

Stargazer Books

© Aladdin Books Ltd 2008

Designed and produced by
Aladdin Books Ltd

First published in 2008
in the United States by
Stargazer Books
c/o The Creative Company
123 South Broad Street
Mankato, Minnesota 56002

Printed in the United States
Illustrator: Lisa Kopper

Photocredits:
All photos from istockphoto.com except 9—comstock

Library of Congress Cataloging-in-Publication Data

Petty, Kate.
  Moving day / by Kate Petty.
      p. cm. -- (My first time)
  Summary: When his family sells their apartment, Sam is not sure
he wants to move, but the experience proves to be exciting and fun.
  Includes index.
   ISBN 978-1-59604-157-8 (alk. paper)
   [1. Moving, Household--Fiction. 2. Family life--Fiction.] I. Title.
PZ7.P44814Md 2007
  [E]--dc22
                    2007001768

About this book

New experiences can be scary for young children. This series will help them to understand situations they may find themselves in, by explaining in a friendly way what can happen.

This book can be used as a starting point for discussing issues. The questions in some of the boxes ask children about their own experiences.

The stories will also help children to master basic reading skills and learn new vocabulary.

It can help if you read the first sentence to children, and then encourage them to read the rest of the page or story. At the end, try looking through the book again to find where the words in the glossary are used.

Contents

There's a big sign outside the apartment where
Sam and Jenny live. It says, "For Sale."

Some people come to see the apartment.
They may want to buy it.

4

Sam and Jenny follow Mom as she shows the visitors around.

They like Sam's room—but so does Sam! He doesn't want strangers sleeping there.

Do you live in a house or an apartment?

Mom and Dad have found a new house.
They take Sam and Jenny to see it.

There's an upstairs and a downstairs
and a backyard.

Outside in the yard Jenny has
found a big, friendly dog.

Can they keep him? No, they can't.
His owners will take him with them.

Sam has almost forgotten about moving,
but this morning a letter arrives.

"We're going to move in three weeks!"
Sam isn't so happy. He likes the apartment.

You can carry pets in a special box.

"Will Kitty come with us?" asks Jenny.
"Of course," says Mom, "she's ours."

Sam wonders about the new backyard. Surely nobody can take that with them!

Now the whole family is very busy.
Everything has to be packed in boxes.

Mom wraps the delicate things carefully
so they don't break when they're moved.

The apartment begins to look very bare
and not a bit like home anymore.

Sam thinks perhaps he won't be sorry
to move to the new house after all.

Today is moving day.
A big van arrives.
The men carry out the furniture.

Sam wonders how they can lift it.
Back and forth, in and out they go.

That looks heavy!

At last everything is neatly packed up.
It's time to follow the van to the
new house. The cat is packed too—
she's safely in her basket. Off they go.

13

"Here we are. Now we can move in. Don't let Kitty out, Jenny," says Mom.

Sam can't wait to get inside and explore the empty rooms.

Would you like to build a new house?

14

The moving men start unloading.
In and out of the house they go again and again.

Sam rushes out to meet the neighbors.
Jenny will have to meet them tomorrow.

At last the van is empty.
The men say goodbye.

The kitchen things are
still packed so Dad
gets a take-out dinner.

A new house has
empty rooms.

16

Jenny wonders where the cat is.
She's safe and sound, but rather angry.

She'd like some food too!

Sam goes upstairs to his very own room.
They've never had an "upstairs" before.

Jenny's fast asleep already.
Dad takes her up to bed.

She's sleeping alone tonight so Dad leaves the door open.

Dad has promised to paint Sam's room. Sam wonders what color to choose.

What color paint would you choose?

Now Sam has gone to sleep too.
Mom and Dad carry on working.

One by one the boxes are unpacked
and the house begins to look like home.

Kitty sniffs and prowls around.

But when Mom and Dad sit down,
Kitty settles between them on the couch.
She has a backyard to explore tomorrow.

"For Sale"
sign

packing

moving van

keys

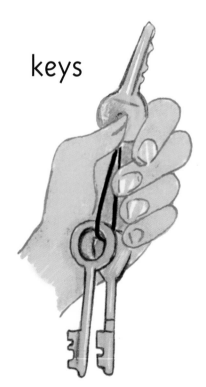

22